OAK TREE TALES

Sip Squippel
Starts a Business

Dorothea King

Sir Squirrel was being most secretive. A few days ago an enormous crate had been delivered to his house and, after that, a team of workmen had arrived with yet more boxes.

For days they had been going up and down the tree carrying pieces of wood, boxes of nails and even a large desk.

Sir Squirrel's friends just couldn't understand what was going on.

"It's always the same," Mistress Hedgehog complained to Miss Mouse as they went shopping. "He always wants to know other people's business but never tells us what he's doing."

Miss Mouse agreed with her. "And for the last week he has done nothing but ask questions about where I've been and who I've seen," she added.

They were just coming out of the baker's shop when they spotted Master Rabbit on the other side of the road. "I wonder if he knows anything about it?" said Mistress Hedgehog.

The rabbit didn't seem to know any more than they did. And what was more, he didn't care. "At least you can't blame me for making all the noise now," he grinned.

Indeed he was right, for there had been so much banging and clanking going on for the last few days that the mouse and the hedgehog had almost complained.

"Expect we will all know soon enough," said the rabbit as he went on his way.

That evening the animals were all outside in the clearing enjoying the warm evening air. Miss Mouse was mending Master Rabbit's shirt while Mistress Hedgehog put yet another patch on his trousers.

"The newspapers these days contain nothing but rubbish," said Sir Squirrel, flicking through his evening paper.

"I read something good last week," said the rabbit.

"You can't read," snorted the hedgehog.

"Well — I looked hard," protested the rabbit.

"Stupid little animal," muttered Mistress Hedgehog.

Sir Squirrel folded his newspaper and gave a sigh. "Rubbish, nothing but rubbish. I could do it better myself."

"Why don't you then?" said Miss Mouse kindly. "You're very good at writing things."

"Well, as a matter-of-fact, that is just my intention," said the squirrel pompously, and stood up placing the newspaper carefully under his arm. "I am proud to announce that tomorrow morning you will all be reading the first edition of the *Oak Tree Times.*"

"You might be," said the rabbit with a yawn. "But not me, I can't read."

"So that's what you've been up to," said Mistress Hedgehog in annoyance.

"Yes, my dear," said Sir Squirrel and pointed to his house. "And up there I have installed a truly marvellous machine."

"Can we come up and see it?" asked Miss Mouse excitedly.

"With pleasure," said Sir Squirrel, and led them up the tree and into his house.

The rabbit was terribly impressed with the large piece of machinery which now almost filled the squirrel's study, and couldn't wait to see it working.

"Ugliest thing I have ever seen," snorted Mistress Hedgehog.

"Yes, but wait and see what it can do," said the squirrel, waving a piece of paper.

Carefully he placed the paper on a kind of tray, slid it into the machine, pulled down a handle and, after a few seconds, was holding a piece of paper covered in words.

"Marvellous, don't you agree?"

The others couldn't help but agree with him, especially the rabbit, who, much to the squirrel's annoyance, was pressing every button and pulling every lever in sight.

Early the following morning the animals all received a copy of the *Oak Tree Times*.

Mistress Hedgehog said the recipe for Surprise Pudding looked so good that she would make it for Sunday lunch, and they were all invited.

Miss Mouse was interested to read that there was going to be a Mouse Ball the following Saturday, with free food afterwards.

The rabbit, not being able to read, used his copy to light a bonfire. So, all-in-all, the animals found it a very useful newspaper.

For the next few days Sir Squirrel was kept very busy, as there were so many events taking place.

Miss Mouse was delighted when she was declared 'Best Dressed Mouse' at the Mouse Ball, and the squirrel wrote a long article on exactly what she had worn. 'Miss Mouse was dressed in a charming creation covered with sequins', he wrote, 'and was the belle of the ball.'

Mistress Hedgehog was pleased to have her name in the newspaper when she was made 'Seamstress of the Year'.

A week later the squirrel reported on 'The Flying Competition', which was won by Witch White. The rabbit *had* taken part with disastrous results, and blamed it on a poor take-off.

In fact the rabbit was the only animal feeling left out. He had certainly *tried* to get his name in the paper. After the 'Flying Competition', he had even invented a machine for slicing carrots. Admittedly it had fallen to bits while he was in the middle of showing Sir Squirrel how it worked. But as he said to the squirrel afterwards, "You could have put something in your paper, such as: 'Rabbit almost invents a machine'."

Sir Squirrel was so cross with the rabbit for wasting his time that he stormed off, leaving him sulking in his workshop.

Two days later, Mistress Hedgehog and Miss Mouse were about to set off on a shopping trip when there was an enormous roar from above.

"Oh dear," sighed Mistress Hedgehog. "What can be the trouble now?"

"Sir Squirrel seems to be really annoyed," said Miss Mouse anxiously.

Suddenly a window was thrown open and Sir Squirrel poked his head out. He was very upset and kept yelling, "I've been robbed! I've been robbed!"

The two animals rushed up the tree.

"Don't come in," yelled Sir Squirrel from the window.

"How can we help if you won't let us in?" snorted Mistress Hedgehog, and went towards the door.

"No, you can't come in," the squirrel shouted. "Someone's stolen all my clothes!"

Mistress Hedgehog and Miss Mouse began to giggle, which upset the squirrel even more.

"Can't you see how serious this is," he yelled.

After a while the mouse and the hedgehog managed to compose themselves and suggested they fetch the local policeman, P.C. Macaul.

Sir Squirrel agreed that it was the only thing they could do, but first would they please find him some clothes.

The rabbit was most obliging and offered his best outfit. None of it fitted too well but Sir Squirrel was too upset to care.

After a while P.C. Macaul arrived and made a long list of all the items which were missing.

"Expect it's them pixies up to their tricks again," he said grimly. "I had trouble with them only last week."

"I want them all punished," said Sir Squirrel angrily. "Every single one of them."

"I will get on to it right away, sir," said P.C. Macaul closing his notebook.

For two days nothing happened and there was still no sign of the squirrel's clothes.

P.C. Macaul had been to see the pixies but they knew nothing about the matter. "Why would we want his clothes?" they said. "None of them would even fit us." P.C. Macaul had to agree that they were somewhat smaller than the squirrel.

On the third day after the robbery Sir Squirrel, Miss Mouse and Mistress Hedgehog were all having tea and discussing the situation when there was a loud knock at the door.

On the doorstep stood the rabbit. Sir Squirrel wasn't too pleased to see him as he had quite enough to worry about without the rabbit making silly remarks.

"What do you want?" he demanded crossly.

"Just a little bit of news for your paper," said the rabbit smugly.

"What news could you have which would possibly interest me?" said the squirrel with a sigh.

"Only that I've found your clothes," grinned the rabbit.

Sir Squirrel was absolutely delighted. "My dear chap, do come in," he said.

The rabbit was most secretive about where he had found the clothes, but said, "It's not very far," and that they should all come and have a look.

Quickly they hurried down the path and out to the field on the edge of the wood.

When they saw what had happened to the squirrel's clothes, Miss Mouse and Mistress Hedgehog began to laugh ... for it really was a funny sight.

There in the field were dozens of scarecrows ... all wearing the squirrel's clothes.

Sir Squirrel was speechless, but nevertheless delighted with the rabbit for finding his clothes.

The following day there was a special edition of the *Oak Tree Times*, and there on the front page was a large headline which read 'RABBIT FINDS MISSING CLOTHES'.

All that day the rabbit went around with an enormous grin on his face. At last he had got his name in the newspaper.

The only person not happy with the news was P.C. Macaul, who was busy doing his own investigations.

That evening the animals were all in the squirrel's house enjoying a celebration drink of blackberry wine, when there was a loud knock on the door.

Outside stood P.C. Macaul carrying a large rule.

"Wonder if I could just have a word with the rabbit, sir?"

The animals were most amazed when P.C. Macaul asked to measure the rabbit's feet. "Just as I thought," he said grimly. "Exactly the same size as the footprints around the scarecrows." He stood up and took the rabbit by the collar. "May I ask you to accompany me to the station, sir?" he said.

"It was only a joke," grinned the rabbit weakly.

Mistress Hedgehog and Miss Mouse both appealed to Sir Squirrel.

"He didn't mean any harm really," whispered Miss Mouse.

"He just gets silly ideas sometimes," added Mistress Hedgehog.

"Oh, very well," said the squirrel crossly. "But he'll not get away with it quite so lightly next time."

When P.C. Macaul had left, the rabbit said how sorry he was about the whole thing.

"But you must admit the scarecrows *did* look funny," he grinned.

Even Sir Squirrel had to admit he was right!